THE MAGIC POND

by Hélène Schweiger

gatekeeper press

Columbus, Ohio

The Magic Pond
Published by Gatekeeper Press
2167 Stringtown Rd, Suite 109
Columbus, OH 43123-2989
www.GatekeeperPress.com

Library of Congress Control Number: 2020947021

ISBN (hardcover): 9781642375220
ISBN (paperback): 9781642375237

eISBN: 9781642375121

Bim bam boom, bada boom, boing, boing, boing.

A big red ball bounced down the stairs towards the front door.

Just as the ball was about to hit the front door, it was opened by Danielka and Jirik's mother.

"What on earth is happening here?" She asked as she brushed the snow off her coat and took off her warm boots.

There was no answer.

As she picked up the red ball, she noticed how heavy it was. She wondered where it came from, as she had never seen it before.

When she looked up the stairs, she could see her daughter.

"Danielka, where is your brother?"

"Right here Mama," answered the little girl as she pointed to her left.

Jirik wasn't there, or at least not the Jirik they knew. Instead, to her left, was the cutest little green frog. It looked as surprised as everyone else.

The frog had the boy's intelligent eyes and cheeky smile.

"Jirik?"

Jirik opened his mouth to answer his mother, but no words came out, only a loud croak.

He put his hands over his mouth, as if to take the sound back. His eyes widened like saucers when he realised that his hands now had four fingers and were green!

Everyone looked astonished.

The red ball suddenly started to vibrate in Mama's hands. The vibration became faster and faster and the ball started to heat up.

Mama put it back down on the floor and cautiously moved away from it. She went up the stairs to be with her twins. Well, with her daughter and a frog.

As Jirik jumped onto Mama's shoulder, Danielka held tightly on to her Mama's arm.

The trio stared down at the ball because they could see something amazing was happening.

The red ball began to transform. It grew and grew until it turned into an elf. She was beautiful. Her long hair shimmered with all the colours of the universe. The most beautiful almond shaped eyes with a deep, rich purple hue peered up at them with a warm and loving smile.

"Hi there, my name is Cuoppu Vaibmu Eana Geassi. You can call me Cuo, it's easier," said the elf, looking quite at ease with the whole situation.

Her voice was melodic. It sounded like crystal chimes caressed by a soft summer breeze. Mama, Danielka, and Jirik were flabbergasted; their mouths opened in shock.

But Danielka was just too curious to stay put.

In silence, she let go of Mama's arm and slowly went down the stairs. When she reached the bottom, she was so close to Cuo that she could actually stroke her robe. The robe was as delicate as a feather. It was also as white as the first powdery snow on the branches of fir trees. She reached up to touch the elf's hand. It was soft and warm.

"Hi, I'm Danielka and this is my Mama and Jirik, my brother. Normally, he doesn't look like this, you know. He's a boy. We are twins. We are six years and nine months old, but I am older by three minutes. I love green you know. What's your favourite colour?"

As Danielka started chattering (when she started to talk, she was unstoppable), Mama went down the stairs too. She didn't really know what to do in the presence of an elf, so she decided to give her a little bow.

"Hello Cuo, my name is Zuzana, but everyone calls me Mama." She said, as she bowed again, feeling very awkward.

Cuo started to laugh.

"There's no need to bow or anything. Would you mind taking me to the kitchen? I'm starving. After 150 years of being locked up in that ball, I'm so looking forward to some nice, hearty food."

"Croak, croak, croaaaak," said Jirik.

Mama looked at him, puzzled.

Danielka dismissed her brother's comment with a shrug of her little shoulders.

"Pff, Jirik, you're scared of any little thing you don't know. Cuo is nice," she asserted firmly.

"Croak?"

"Yes, trust me."

"Croak."

Danielka giggled. Jirik always had a funny comment to make.

The small party settled down in the cosy kitchen, where the tea was brewing, and the scones were warming gently on the stove.

Cuo could sense how very curious the trio was.

"As I've told you, my name is Cuo. I've slept for 150 years and I'm 192 years old. We stop ageing when we sleep, which is pretty cool, right? What's happening to Jirik isn't exactly normal, but I'm sure you know this already!"

Danielka and Jirik couldn't hold back their questions any longer.

"But" "Croak" "How?" "Croak" "WHEN? "CROAK?"

"Stop it both of you! You're always speaking at the same time, it's really annoying. Jirik, you go first. Danielka, you translate and don't make any comments," said Mama firmly.

Jirik puffed up his chest, he felt very proud to be the first one to ask questions.

Danielka did as Mama said and didn't comment once, although she was dying to.

"Last night, it was full moon. I noticed the stars were shining brightly, as if a light had been turned on inside them. I know I'm not allowed to, but I went outside to the pond," said Jirik, his little frog face pleading for understanding. "It was really strange. The stars reflected in the pond weren't the same ones that were in the sky, so I threw a stone in the water to see what would happen. The ripples didn't ripple! Mama, they didn't ripple!"

A silence fell over the kitchen. Something odd was happening for sure.

Danielka asked whether, at long last, she was allowed to speak. Mama nod her agreement smiling at her daughter's eagerness.

"I knew Jirik was outside, so I followed him," she stuck her tongue out at the little frog. "I'm not scared of the dark either! I just wanted to know what you were doing," she continued, pouting. "As I was crossing the lawn, I saw something amazing. From the pond, a sort of veil lifted and floated up to the sky. It touched Jirik and he turned into a frog and then the red ball appeared. I ran to the pond and picked both of them up. And then, I rushed back home as quickly as I could and hid under my duvet. I was sure it was just a bad dream but this morning."

Cuo understood at once what had happened and started to explain.

"Every 150 years, when the star Aldebaran is directly above the pond and there is a full moon, an energy void opens up. It allows elves, gnomes, and fairies to regain their strength and for the wisdom of the universe to be shared. This only lasts a few seconds, but it feels like an eternity. It's such a wonderful feeling! Because Jirik was at the pond at that exact moment, he was transformed into a frog so he could be protected from all that energy!"

"Croak, croak, croak," croaked Jirik alarmingly, his croak getting louder and louder to the point that all the others covered their ears.

"Does that mean that Jirik needs to wait another 150 years before he can become a boy again?" Gasped Danielka and Mama.

"No, no, no! We can do something about it tomorrow. In the meantime, you should all go to bed and get some rest. All these emotions have completely worn you out," soothed Cuo.

"Don't you want to rest too?" Asked Mama, a little worried.

"I just slept for 150 years!" Said Cuo with a big smile.

Cuo was deep in thought when she heard a tap on the window.

When she turned around, she instantly recognised a dear old friend.

"Pikomo! What a wonderful surprise! What are you doing here?" Exclaimed Cuo, her smile shining with delight.

"Hello Cuo! How are you? Did you manage to get yourself into trouble again?" Asked Pikomo with a wink.

Cuo knelt on the floor so that she could hug her friend.

Pikomo was no elf. He was a creature of the universe. He had the torso and arms of a man, long legs of a frog and wings of a dragon. To top it all off, he had an otter's head, which was very handsome. He was also a Wise One. His life extended over many times and realms.

"So, what has happened here? You know we don't like our world to interfere with humans. Nothing good ever comes of it," enquired Pikomo, scratching his forehead.

"In all truth, this really is a case of being in the wrong place at the wrong time," answered Cuo thoughtfully. "I remember reading somewhere in one of my textbooks that there is a way to solve this," she continued, looking at Pikomo with hopeful eyes.

"Yes, there is a way and quite a simple one too. But we must act while the night is still on our side. By tomorrow morning, this whole situation must have been dealt with, as though it had never happened."

"Is that possible? I mean, Jirik will always remember being a frog, won't he? And Danielka has a vivid imagination."

"Jirik needs to be part of the ceremony otherwise it cannot work. Here's how we'll proceed," interrupted Pikomo.

He started to jump around the kitchen while explaining the plan to Cuo.

She couldn't help but smile. She still remembered the first time she had encountered him.

He had been giving a lecture on the benefits of sweet algae in magic potions. The class couldn't concentrate because he kept jumping all over the place. He couldn't help it, jumping helped him think better.

In the end, one student dared to raise a hand and asked him if he could try and stay in one place. His answer had been a memorable one, and a lesson in itself.

"Well, if you can't concentrate when I'm jumping around, what will you do when you are facing a mortal enemy? Ask him to stand still while you think?" That got all the students to concentrate.

"Sorry Pikomo, I wasn't listening," apologised Cuo.

"Yes, I can see that you always were a daydreamer. So, here's the plan: you and I will go to the pond right now. We need to collect seven different coloured items: red, orange, yellow, green, blue, violet and purple. Our friends from the pond will play an important role as we must sing each colour's magic words. You remember them, right?" Asked Pikomo.

"Of course," answered Cuo quickly. She was frantically racking her brain to remember them all.

"Okay, so when everything is in place, you'll go and get Jirik."

"His mother and sister too?" asked Cuo.

"No, only Jirik. The less the others see, the better. Anyway, we want them to think that this was all a dream. When Jirik is with us, here's what will happen. As we chant each item's magic words, an arch with seven branches will rise above the pond. Jirik will have to repeat the seven sentences three times. Those magic words will become part of him and give him inner strength. Then he'll croak as loudly as he possibly can. His croak will shatter the arch into a million enchanted pieces, which will fall on him, making him a little boy again. You'll then take him back to bed. Once you're back at the pond, we'll all resume our lives as if nothing had happened."

"Will this work?" Asked Cuo doubtfully.

"Of course it will, it's not the first time we've had to do this. If you'd taken the refresher course like you should have, then you'd know this Mademoiselle Cuo!"

"Right, okay. So, this is my cue to go and get the stuff, right?" Sang Cuo as she hurried away from Pimoko's frown.

When they arrived at the pond with all of the items, they heard the sound of hushed discussions.

"Oh really? A human was here?"

"An elf is captive? Oh noooo! What will we do?"

Through the branches and bushes, Cuo and Pikomo saw that the pond's creatures looked agitated and scared. They believed their sanctuary was no longer safe.

Pikomo jumped right into the middle of this frenzy and addressed the assembly in a commanding voice.

"Listen to me my friends. There is nothing to be afraid of. There is a standard procedure and we will follow it." He held his breath before puffing with annoyance. "If you had all done your homework, then you'd know this, and you would not get in a state over something silly. So, I need seven of you in front of me NOW!"

As the seven volunteers came forward, Cuo gave them each an item and said the corresponding magic words.

The toad was given the red pen and the magic words.

"I am safe."

The dragonfly was given the orange cup and the words,

"I am alive."

The otter was given the yellow sock and the words,

"I am confident in all I do."

The duck was given the green scarf and the words,

"I love myself and others."

The freshwater shrimp was given the blue ribbon and the words,

"I speak the truth."

The snail was given the violet glove and the words,

"I am guided by my inner wisdom."

And, finally, the turtle was given the purple hat and the magic words,

"I am at peace."

When all the items had been handed out, Pikomo reminded them of the next steps.

"Cuo will go and get Jirik. While she does this, you'll all take your places around the pond. When they get back, Jirik and Cuo will climb on the water lily and sail to the middle of the pond. On my signal, starting with you, my friend the toad, we will chant the magic words. Then, going clockwise we will do the same for the remaining colours. At the end, we will chant the seven sentences one last time. The energy will start to flow and create the magical arch." Pikomo looked around to see if they all were following what he was saying.

Cuo finished the explanation.

"While I bring Jirik to the pond, I'll reassure him that we're here to help. I'll share with him the seven magical sentences and explain what he needs to do. When the time is right for him to croak,

I'll let you know. You'll have to cover your ears – it'll be SUPER loud."

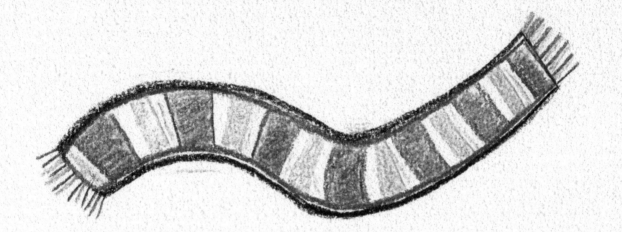

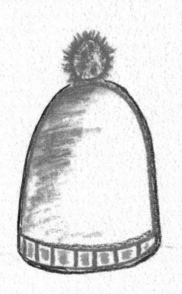

Up in the house, no one was finding it easy to sleep.

Mama couldn't help but play the last moments of the day over and over in her mind. She wondered whether she'd dreamt it all.

In the room next door, Danielka tossed and turned in her little red bed. She sighed once more and finally got up.

"Jirik? Are you sleeping?" She asked as she shook her brother's frog legs. "I'm not sleepy at all," she continued.

"Oh Danielka, what if Cuo doesn't know what to do?" Croaked Jirik worriedly. "I want to be a little boy again," he finished, and started to cry.

Mama could hear her twins whispering. She got up and joined them in the room they shared.

"Come my children, let's sleep together tonight. It's been a very weird day," she said with her arms open wide.

They climbed into her big wooden bed and Mama sang them a lullaby. Very soon, both children were fast asleep. Mama also started to feel her eyes getting heavier. In the end, she fell asleep too, having dreams full of fairies and magic.

Cuo stood guard in front of the house, using her super hearing powers to know when the household was asleep.

As soon as she heard everyone's steady breathing, punctuated by some muffled croaks, she came into the room and very delicately took Jirik in her arms.

He woke up with a start and was about to give the croak of his life when he realised that he was in Cuo's arms. His heart calmed down slightly. As he was about to open his mouth, Cuo shushed him.

"Stay quiet my friend. I'll explain everything when we're outside. We mustn't wake your mother and sister."

As quietly as the flight of a blue jay, they left the house.

Cuo described to Jirik how he'd change back into a little boy again and what would happen afterwards.

"Jirik, this whole situation should never have happened. Normally our worlds don't meet. When the ceremony is over and you're back to your joyful self, you'll remember what took place for only a little while. In a couple of days, no one in your family will remember what happened."

"Really? You'll erase our memory?" Interrupted Jirik worriedly.

"No, no. Any magic that shouldn't have happened slowly disappears from a human's memory. This way, you can continue to live a happy life without having to keep secrets. Do you understand?"

"Yes," said Jirik thoughtfully. "Will we forget you? Danielka will be sad. She likes you a lot you know."

"You'll remember this as a very vivid dream. It's always cool to have nice dreams don't you think?"

"Yes, I like nice dreams," smiled Jirik.

By now, they had reached their destination.

All the pond creatures were there, ready to help Jirik. He could feel the positive energy and wasn't scared at all when he met Pikomo.

"Hello Jirik, are you ready to repeat the sentences and give the croak that will free you from your current predicament?" Asked Pikomo.

"My what?" Jirik looked at him blankly. Cuo giggled.

"What Pikomo is asking is whether you're ready to give it your best shot to become a boy again?"

"CROAK," answered Jirik beaming.

Pikomo smiled and lifted both hands in the air to get everyone's attention.

"On my signal, toad, you'll start."

He lowered his hands and the big toad began chanting the magic words. As soon as he started, a red light began to shine where he was standing. The red light became stronger and stronger until it rose up into the night.

Then the dragonfly chanted his magic words and the orange light rose up. The yellow followed soon after, then the green, then the blue, the violet and lastly, the purple. All the lights were rising up into the night sky. They met at a single point right above the pond.

It was absolutely beautiful. It shone iridescent, full of life and energy. Jirik's eyes were about to pop out of his head in amazement.

"Come, let's get to the middle of the pond," said Cuo encouragingly.

They climbed onto a magnificent enchanted water lily that glided them to the middle of the pond, as though they were being pulled by a magic thread.

When Cuo and Jirik arrived at the middle of the pond, they gazed upwards, and what they saw was magical.

"Oh wow, I've never seen it! I've only heard of it," exclaimed Cuo, awestruck. Jirik had lost all power of speech.

Above their heads was a circle, its rim was shimmering gold. Inside, the seven colours were dancing and changing shape every second, like a living painting. Jirik saw a dragon, the tail of a whale, and children chasing each other. Jirik and Cuo were totally mesmerised by the sight.

"Right, Jirik, it's time," said Cuo, gently bringing him back to reality. "Take a deep breath, repeat the sentences and croak as many times as you want and as loudly as you can. Don't hold back. Okay?"

Jirik nodded his head, understanding what he needed to do.

He took a deep breath and repeated the sentences three times: "I am safe, I am alive, I am confident in all I do, I love myself and others, I speak the truth, I am guided by my inner wisdom, I am at peace."

Then he filled up his frog cheeks so much that they looked like two balloons about to burst and at last, he let out the loudest

"CROAK!"

At the sound, the arch above the pond shattered into a million tiny pieces that were as light as feathers.

They fell slowly, like snowflakes. As they landed softly on Jirik, his body changed back into that of a little boy.

Minutes later, the pond fell quiet. No one dared to breath or make any noise.

Pikomo brought everyone out of their trance when he flew to the middle of the pond to check on Jirik and Cuo.

"Are you okay there?"

"Yes. Look, it worked!" Announced Cuo happily.

Jirik looked at himself. His fingers, his legs, his feet. He put his hands in his hair to make sure he was no longer bald like a frog. He was so relieved!

"Very good. Now you must rush back home. Take all the items with you and do not say a word to anyone," said Pikomo firmly.

Cuo and Jirik did as they were told and rushed back to the house. Jirik was so happy, it felt like he was flying home.

When they arrived, they were both out of breath. Softly, they opened the door. Jirik dumped the scarf and the other items on the floor. He just wanted to run to the big bed and fall back to sleep with his mother and twin sister.

"Bye Jirik," murmured Cuo, ruffling his hair. "You take care of yourself now. Have a wonderful life. Continue to be curious, continue to be daring, continue to ask questions, continue to be open to magic and remember the seven sentences – they will give you strength throughout your whole life."

Jirik embraced Cuo's legs tightly and muffled a few words into her robe.

"Thank you so much for helping me and Pikomo and the creatures from the pond too. I'll always have nice dreams about you! Can I share the sentences with Danielka?"

Cuo leaned down and gave him a soft kiss on the forehead.

"Of course you can, and with whomever else you want to and for the rest of your life! These words are magic, and everyone should know them in their heart. May love and magic be with you always, my little friend."

Jirik ran up to the bedroom where he found his mother and sister fast asleep as if nothing had happened.
He squeezed himself back into the bed between them. He felt warm and safe there.

The next morning, when they woke up, they looked at each other in bewilderment.

Mama and Danielka were over the moon when they realised Jirik was back to his normal self.

Mama even started to question whether this whole thing had actually happened. But she soon got distracted when she noticed the mess downstairs.

"Kids, you clean this mess up while I cook a nice breakfast. Who wants pancakes?"

"We do!" Answered both Danielka and Jirik happily.

When Mama entered the kitchen and looked out of the window, she called for the twins to come quickly.

"Look over at the pond, there's a beautiful rainbow," she said, holding each twin tightly by her side. "Let's have breakfast my darlings and enjoy a beautiful day together."

From behind the grass and bushes, Cuo and Pikomo waved them goodbye and wished them good luck.

The End

About the Author

After many years in corporate life, Hélène decided to take the plunge and do what she has always wanted to do – write stories for children.

Hélène is French and Danish. She has lived in many countries in Europe. She has two cats who closely monitor when she is available for cuddles and playtime. She loves nature and sees beauty everywhere. Her motto is 'there is a silver lining to every cloud'.

There is no limit to her imagination. She uses storytelling on a daily basis as a perfect way to convey messages to children and adults.

Hélène wants to share universal messages to all children in the world, to give them the strength to become the wonderful adults they can be.

CPSIA information can be obtained
at www.ICGtesting.com
Printed in the USA
LVHW072317290321
682890LV00023B/1114

9 781642 375220